To Terra,
Happy Birthday,

all BEST WISHES
Will Hmmm
2004
TLA

DOWN ON THE FARM

by Merrily Kutner

illustrated by Will Hillenbrand

Holiday House / New York

Library of Congress Cataloging-in-Publication Data
Kutner, Merrily.
Down on the farm / by Merrily Kutner ; illustrated by Will
Hillenbrand.—1st ed.
p. cm.
Summary: Simple rhyming text describes the sounds and activities
of animals during a day on the farm.
ISBN 0-8234-1721-2 (hardcover)
[1. Farm life—Fiction. 2. Domestic animals—Fiction. 3. Animal sounds—
Fiction. 4. Stories in rhyme.] I. Hillenbrand, Will, ill. II. Title.
PZ8.3.K965Do2004
[E]—dc21
2003050815

For my precious daughter, Marisa—
in loving memory
M. K.

To Sheri Woodward,
down on the farm
W. H.

Sun comes up.
KiD WaKe☺ uP!
Down on the farm,
DOWN ON THE FARM.

Crows peck straw—
CAW, CAW, CAW.
Down on the farm,
DOWN ON THE FARM.

Cows will chew—
Moo, Moo, Moo.
Down on the farm,
DOWN ON THE FARM.

"Ducks, come back!"
QUACK, QUACK, QUACK.
Down on the farm,
DOWN ON THE FARM.

Geese kerplonk—
HONK, HONK, HONK.
Down on the farm,
DOWN ON THE FARM.

Turkeys squabble—
GOBBLE, GOBBLE, GOBBLE.
Down on the farm,
DOWN ON THE FARM.

Dog's on roof—
WOOF, WOOF, WOOF.
Down on the farm,
DOWN ON THE FARM.

Pig snouts point—
OiNK. OiNK. OiNK.
Down on the farm,
DOWN ON THE FARM.

Goats repeat,
"BLeaT, BLeaT, BLeaT."
Down on the farm,
DOWN ON THE FARM.

Sheep graze far—
Baa. Baa. Baa.

Down on the farm,
DOWN ON THE FARM.

Chicks won't sleep—
PeeP. PeeP. PeeP.
Down on the farm,
DOWN ON THE FARM.

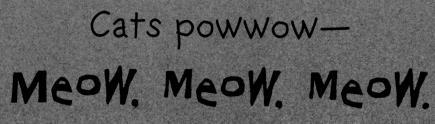

Cats powwow—
MeoW, MeoW, MeoW.
Down on the farm,
DOWN ON THE FARM.

Sun goes down.
SHH!
QUIET TOWN.
Down on the farm,
DOWN ON
THE FARM.